This wonderful book belongs to:

We're Molly Muddle, Polly and Skip
Ruby, TomTom, Bubble and Pip
welcome to **Our Wonderful World.**

For Camilla - A.B. and S.M.

This edition published 2004. ISBN: 1 904827 02 0

A CIP catalogue record for this book is available from the British Library.

Printed in Singapore

Keppel Publishing Limited
The Grey House, Kenbridge Road
New Galloway, DG7 3RP Scotland.

Molly Muddle's Cake

Anne Butler and Sue Mayfield

Illustrated by Moira Munro

In our wonderful world
is a wonderful house...

...And in the wonderful house Molly Muddle is baking a cake.

Polly and Skip are helping. Molly Muddle puts butter and sugar in a big bowl and stirs. Round and round, round and round. Then she puts in eggs and flour. The flour makes Skip sneeze! A-tish-oo!

Molly Muddle stirs the cake until it is creamy like custard.

"Butter, sugar, eggs and flour," she says to herself, "I'm sure I've forgotten something."

Molly Muddle thinks hard, and just in time she remembers. "Baking powder!" she says. "To make my cake bouncy and fluffy."

Molly Muddle puts in one spoonful of baking powder.

"Only one," she says. "That's all it needs."

Molly Muddle stirs the cake, just as the doorbell rings. DING-DONG!

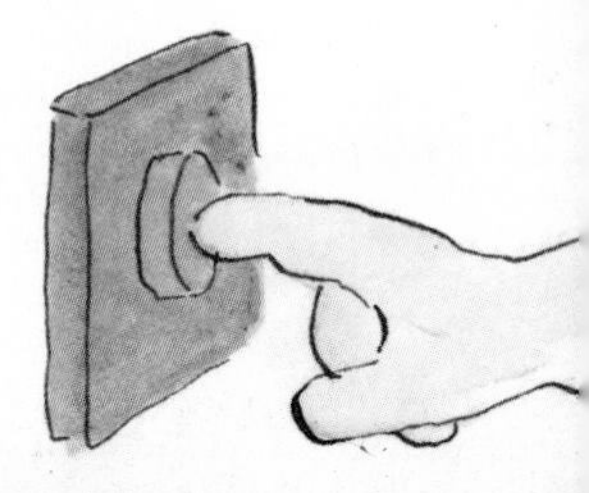

It is Ruby. Ruby has painted a picture of an enormous balloon.

"It's lovely!" says Molly Muddle "Let's put it on the wall. Then I must finish making my cake."

“Now where was I?” Molly Muddle says. “I was just about to add baking powder to make the cake all bouncy and fluffy.”

Molly Muddle adds a spoonful …

…just as the doorbell rings. DING-DONG!

It is TomTom. "Listen to this!" he says. TomTom has made up a song. He sings his song and plays his drum.

"See me zoom! Round the room! Bang-bang-Boom! Bang-bang-Boom!"

Molly Muddle and Ruby love the song. And so does Skip. They all dance round and round. Skip zooms.

"That's a wonderful song, TomTom," says Molly Muddle, "But I'm out of breath now!"

"And you need to finish your cake," says Ruby.

With all that dancing Molly Muddle has forgotten what she was doing.

"Did I put in the baking powder or not?" she asks Skip.

Skip looks at Molly Muddle. "Woof!" he says.

Molly Muddle can't remember so she puts in another spoonful...

...just as the doorbell rings. DING-DONG!

It is Bubble. Bubble has been picking strawberries.

"Delicious!" says Molly Muddle, taking a big juicy strawberry and popping it into her mouth.

"Have another one," says Bubble.

"You could put your strawberries on Molly Muddle's cake," says Ruby.

"My cake!" says Molly Muddle suddenly. "I need to put it in the oven."

Molly Muddle stirs the cake. Did she put in baking powder to make it bouncy and fluffy? Did she or didn't she? What a muddle!

Molly Muddle thinks for a moment. Dear me, she isn't sure!

So she adds two spoonfuls just in case and pops the cake in the oven.

The doorbell rings again.
DING-DONG!

Ding dong bell,
ding dong bell!

It is Pip. "Come and see this!" says Pip and they all go out into the garden.

There, on a big blue flower, is a beautiful butterfly.

"What lovely colours," says Ruby.

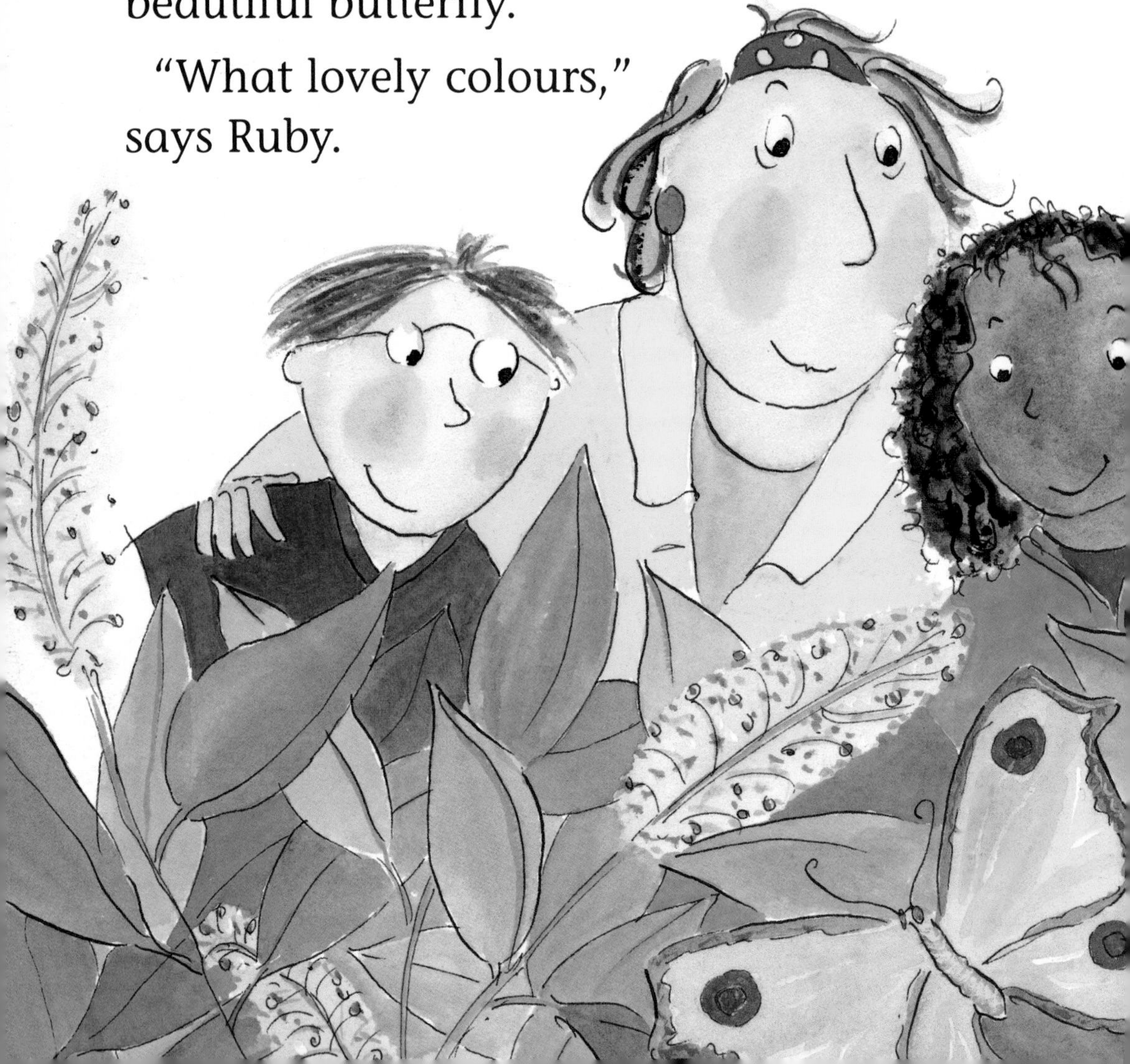

“What lovely spots,” says TomTom.

“Isn’t it a wonderful butterfly?” says Pip. They look at it for a long long time until it flies off.

“I think it’s time for tea,” Molly Muddle says. “My cake will be ready now.”

“I can smell it!” says Bubble. “Yummy yummy!”

Molly Muddle walks towards the house. But, oh dear, what does she see? Something creamy and fluffy is gurgling out of the door and down the step.

"What's that?" shouts Ruby.

"It looks like my cake!" says Molly Muddle.

"Oh no!" Pip says. "What's happened to it?"

Molly Muddle has put in too much baking powder and her cake has bubbled out of the tin...

...out of the oven...

...all the way across the kitchen floor...and out of the door!

Skip licks up the cake. He likes it very much. The more Skip eats, the bouncier he gets. He bounces and bounces all over the garden.

"Look at Skip," says TomTom. "He's all bouncy and fluffy!"

Boing!

Everyone laughs but Molly Muddle is sad because now there is no cake for her friends.

"Never mind," says Pip. "We'll help to make another one."

So they do. Ruby puts in butter. Bubble puts in eggs. TomTom puts in sugar. Pip puts in flour.

And last of all, very, very carefully, Molly Muddle adds one spoonful of baking powder. Only one.

Only one!
Only one!

When the cake is baked, Bubble puts the strawberries on top.

"Look," says Ruby. "There's a strawberry for each of us. Molly Muddle, Polly and Skip, Ruby, TomTom, Bubble and Pip!"

4. Once baked, remove the cakes from the tins, peel off the greaseproof paper and leave to cool.

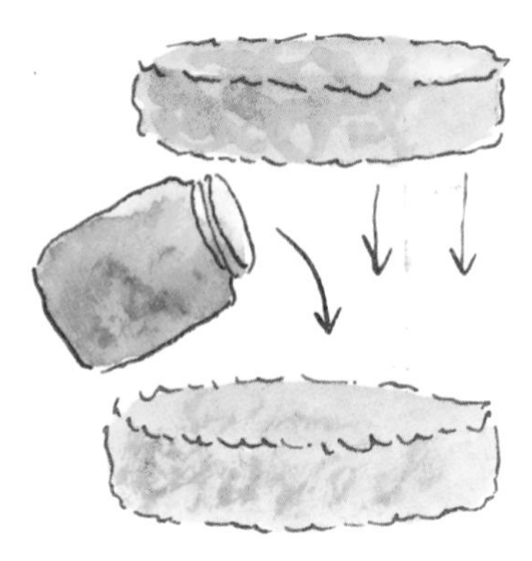

5. When cool, sandwich the cakes together with strawberry jam.

6. Melt the white chocolate in a bowl. Cool down, then stir in the cream cheese and beat well.

7. Spread the topping over the cake and decorate with your favourite fresh fruit.

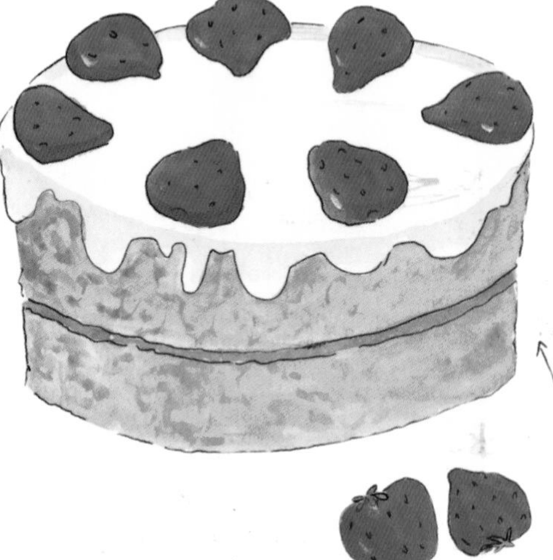

8. Share with your friends!

Make your own wonderful cake

Here's what you need:
100g (4 oz) butter or soft margarine
100g (4 oz) caster sugar
100g (4 oz) self-raising flour
1 small level teaspoon of baking powder (Only one!)
2 large eggs
A few drops vanilla essence

Strawberry jam
100g white chocolate
50g soft cream cheese
Fresh strawberries, grape or satsuma segments.

Here's what to do:

1. Put the butter or margarine, sugar, baking powder, eggs and vanilla essence in a bowl together, sieve in the flour and stir well.

2. Grease two 20 cm (8 inch) cake tins and line with greaseproof paper, then pour the mixture evenly into each tin.

3. Bake in the centre of a pre-heated oven at mark 3/ 325°F/170°C for 25-30 mins.

Everyone says it is a wonderful cake, the best they have ever tasted.

And Skip agrees!